DUCK ON

By David

THE BLUE SKY PRESS

A BIKE

Shannon

An Imprint of Scholastic Inc. • New York

THE BLUE SKY PRESS

For information regarding
permission, please write to:
Permissions Department, Scholastic Inc.,
555 Broadway, New York, New York 10012.
SCHOLASTIC, THE BLUE SKY PRESS,
and associated logos are trademarks and/or
registered trademarks of Scholastic Inc.
Library of Congress catalog card number: 2001035992
ISBN 0-439-05023-5
10 9 8 7 6 5 4 3 2 1   02 03 04 05 06
Printed in Singapore   46
First printing, April 2002

One day down on the farm, Duck got a wild idea. "I bet I could ride a bike!" he thought. He waddled over to where the boy parked his bike, climbed on, and began to ride. At first he rode very slowly, and he wobbled a lot, but it was fun!

Duck rode past Cow and waved to her.
"Hello, Cow!" said Duck.
"M-o-o-o," said Cow. But what she thought was,
"A duck on a bike? That's the silliest thing
I've ever seen!"

Then Duck rode past Sheep.

"Hello, Sheep!" said Duck.

"B-a-a-a," said Sheep. But what she thought was,

"He's going to hurt himself if he's not careful!"

Duck was riding better now.
He rode past Dog.
"Hello, Dog!" said Duck.
"Woof!" said Dog. But what he thought was,
"That is a mighty neat trick!"

Then Duck rode past Cat.

"Hello, Cat!" said Duck.

"Meow," said Cat. But what she thought was,

"I wouldn't waste my time riding a bike!"

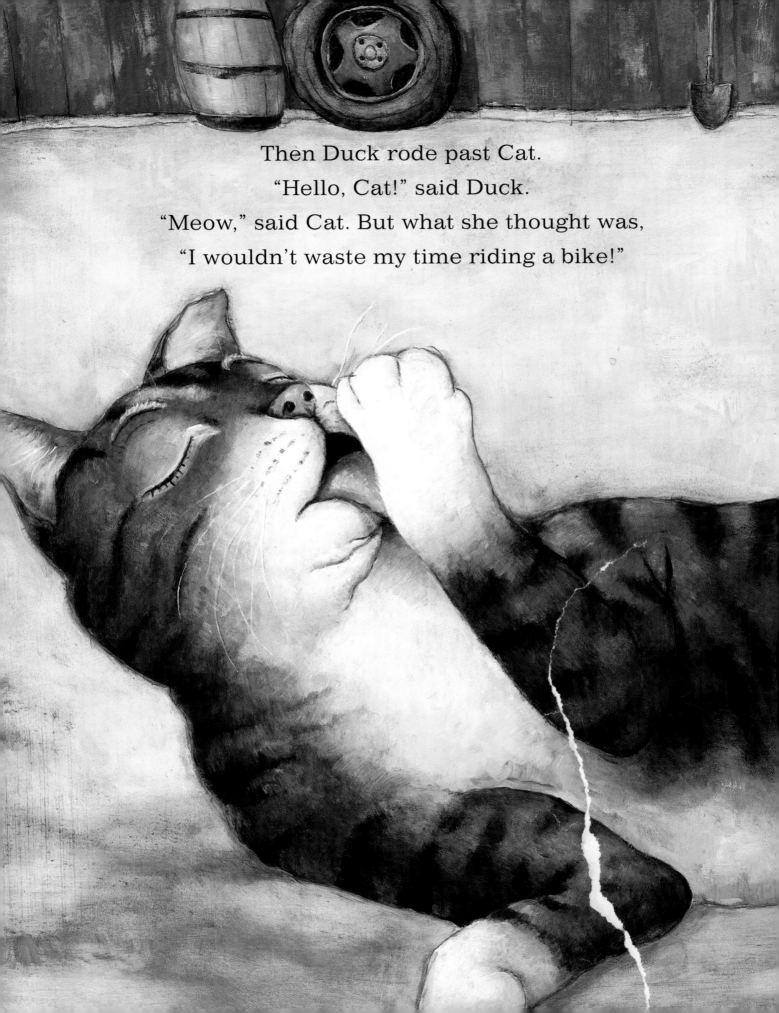

Duck pedaled a little faster.
He rode past Horse.
"Hello, Horse!" said Duck.
"Ne-e-e-igh!" said Horse.
But what he thought was,
"You're still not as fast as me, Duck!"

Duck rang his bell as he rode toward Chicken.
"Hello, Chicken!" said Duck.
"Cluck! Cluck!" said Chicken. But what she thought was,
"Watch where you're going, Duck!"

Then Duck rode past Goat.
"Hello, Goat!" said Duck.
"M-a-a-a," said Goat. But what he thought was,
"I'd like to eat that bike!"

Duck stood on the seat
and rode past Pig and Pig.
"Hello, Pigs!" said Duck.
"Oink," said Pig and Pig.
But what they thought was,
"Duck is such a show-off!"

Then Duck rode no-hands past Mouse.
"Hello, Mouse!" said Duck.
"Squeak," said Mouse. But what he thought was,
"I wish I could ride a bike just like Duck."

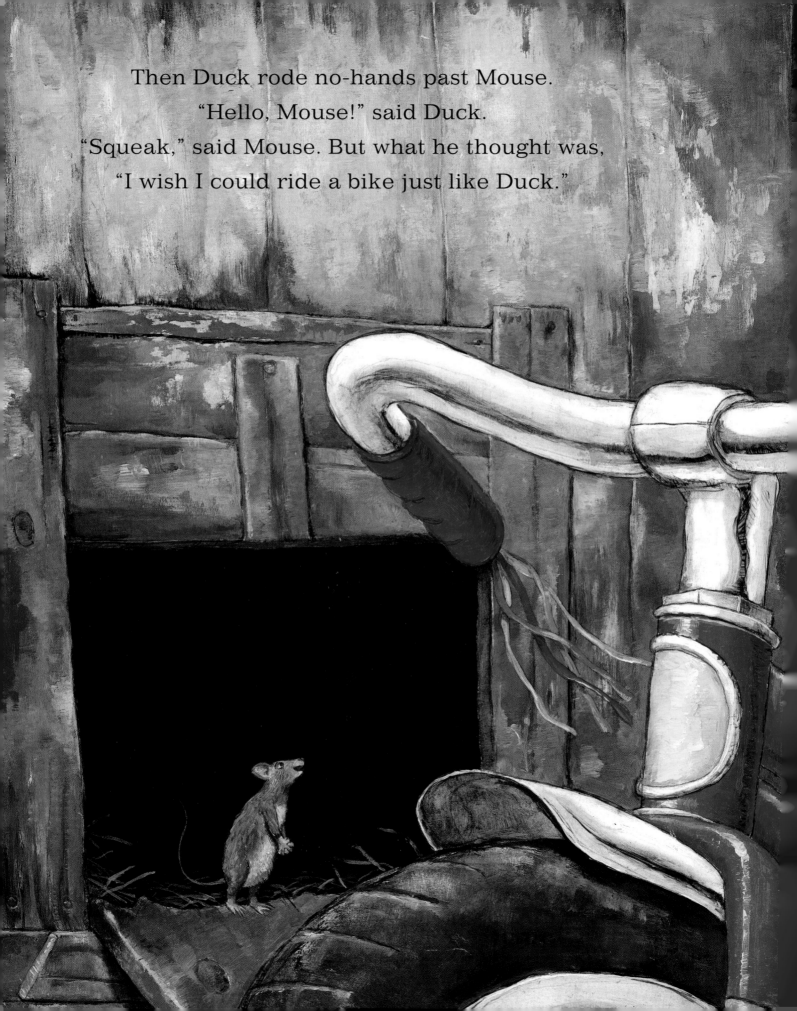

Suddenly, a whole bunch
of kids came down the road on
bikes. They were in such a hurry
that they didn't see Duck.
They parked their bikes by
the house and went inside.

Now all the animals had bikes! They rode
around and around the barnyard.
"This is fun!" they all said.
"Good idea, Duck!"

Then they put the bikes back by the house. And no one
knew that on that afternoon, there had been a cow,
a sheep, a dog, a cat, a horse, a chicken, a goat,
two pigs, a mouse, and a duck on a bike.